BENNY BUNNY'S
NEW
BOOK

BY DEB JOHNSON

 FriesenPress

One Printers Way
Altona, MB R0G 0B0
Canada

www.friesenpress.com

ISBN
978-1-03-914992-2 (Hardcover)
978-1-03-914991-5 (Paperback)
978-1-03-914993-9 (eBook)

1. JUVENILE FICTION, ANIMALS, RABBITS

Distributed to the trade by The Ingram Book Company

With a lifetime of love! To my children: Grant, Nancy, Lisa, and Peter.

Benny Bunny got a new book for his birthday. But Benny is too little to read it. Who will read it to him?

"Mother, will you read my new book to me?"

But Mother says, "No, Benny, I'm sorry but I can't. I'm too busy cooking."

"Grandpa, will you read to me?"

"I'm sorry, Benny," says Grandpa. "I'm too old. My eyes can't read without my glasses, and I can't find my glasses."

"Mr. Owl, will you read to me?"

"Who-o-o?" says Mr. Owl. "No-o-o, I am too tired. Who-o-o."

"Percy Pig, will you read to me?"

Percy Pig is so busy eating, he hardly has time to say to Benny, "No," *gulp*, "I'm too hungry to read."

"Phoebe Fawn, will you read to me?"

Phoebe Fawn is too shy. She does not even answer Benny but hurries off into the forest.

"Morris Mouse, will you read to me?"

"Oh, no! Br-r-r-r! I'm too cold. Br-r-r-r! I fell into the river and now I'm freezing! Br-r-r-r!"

Benny asks the Squirrel Sisters if they will read to him, but they are having too much fun playing.

"Would you read to me?" Benny calls to the Bluebirds. But they are too high and cannot even hear him.

Perhaps Mr. Skunk will have time to read to Benny. But Mr. Skunk says, "I'm sorry, little bunny, but I have too far to go before it gets dark."

"Daisy Duck, will you read to me?"

"I'm sorry, Benny. I'm too wet. I've been splashing and swimming in the pond. If I touch your book, I'll get it all wet and ruin it."

"Will you read to me, Andy Ant?"

But Andy Ant can't read the new book to Benny because he is too small.

Bruce Bear asks, "Would you like me to read to you, Benny?"

But Benny says, "Oh, no! You are TOO big! I'm afraid of you!" And he runs away home.

Poor Benny. No one to read his new book to him. Everyone is too busy, or too old, or too hungry, or too SOMEthing! And his new book looks SO interesting!

Then Mother comes to say, "Benny, I'm all done cooking for now. I have time read to you."

Grandpa says, "I've found my glasses, Benny. Would you like me to read to you now?"

Mr. Owl flies down and hoots, "Who-o-o! I had a very good sleep, Benny, and now I will read to you."

Percy Pig hurries over. "I had a very big dinner, Benny, and I'm not hungry anymore. I'll be happy to read your book to you."

Phoebe Fawn is still too shy, but she would like to hear the story, too.

Morris Mouse says, "Benny, I've been sitting in the warm sun, and I'm nice and dry and warm. Shall I read to you now?"

The Squirrel Sisters have scampered over to hear the story too. They are tired of playing.

The Bluebirds would like to listen, too. And Mr. Skunk is too tired to walk any further, so he would like to read to Benny.

Daisy Duck is all dried off and has come to read to Benny as well.

Even Andy Ant, who is too small to read, is not too small to listen.

Then Bruce Bear growls, "I am big, Benny, but I won't hurt anyone. And since I'm the biggest, I'll read to everyone."

So he does, and everyone listens. And it is a very good story, too!

CPSIA information can be obtained
at www.ICGtesting.com
Printed in the USA
BVHW061421040822
643769BV00003B/34